First published in 1997
by Macdonald Young Books

This edition published in 2009 by Wayland



A catalogue record for this book is available from
the British Library.

ISBN: 978 0 7502 5751 0

Printed in China

Wayland
338 Euston Road, London NW1 3BH

Wayland is a division of Hachette Children's Books,
an Hachette UK Company
www.hachette.co.uk

# Nightwing Towers

LAURENCE STAIG

*Illustrated by Doffy Weir*

WAYLAND

*To Jude, Freya and Edmund.*

# *Chapter One*

Charlie Parsons did not recognize his Great-aunt Sybil when he stepped out of the railway station. He remembered his aunt as a fun-loving, jolly woman with a booming voice, who always wore bright clothes and unusual hats.

But now she looked pale and thin and frighteningly strange with her dark glasses and a thick woolly scarf. She wasn't the same person at all.

"It's not a long walk to Nightwing Towers," she said softly, stooping down for him to give her a peck on the cheek. "Though I do get very tired these days."

Together, they walked through the deserted streets of the Belladonna Housing Estate. Spider-web cracks stretched from the corners of grey, empty windows, gardens were overgrown. In the distance, Charlie could see demolition trucks and cranes. Almost all of the tower blocks had been pulled down. Occasionally, clouds of dust rose like billowing mushrooms.

"The whole place has to go," said Great-aunt Sybil, her voice almost a whisper. "I'm afraid my brand new little bungalow isn't ready yet."

“Not to worry, Aunty,” said Charlie rather nervously. “I’ve never spent a holiday in a high rise block of flats before. I bet you have a great view of London!”

They turned a corner and stopped before a parade of shops. All were deserted, except for a newsagent’s set in the middle.

“Wait here, Aunty,” said Charlie. “I’ll only be a moment.” He wondered if she still had her sweet tooth; perhaps an ice-cream would cheer her up?

He stepped inside the shop.

A small girl wearing a grubby baseball hat, shorts and trainers, stood beside the counter. She was unwrapping a choc-ice but looked deadly serious. Suddenly, she pulled a small yellow card out of the wrapper and read it.

"Is that the one, Freya?" asked the man behind the counter, as he leant forward to look at the card.

She shook her head angrily. "No, and I'm running out of time!"

She took a big bite out of her choc-ice and stormed past Charlie.

"Hey!" said Charlie as he was pushed aside.

"Don't mind Freya," said the shopkeeper. "She's trying to collect the entire Dracula's Delight series. I think it's turned her head!"

He pointed at a poster on the wall. It read:

Charlie screwed up his nose. "Perhaps *I* should try this Dracula's Delight – two please."

Charlie unwrapped the ice-creams which were shaped like wooden stakes. He hurriedly glanced at the cards and put them into his pocket.

Outside, his aunt was standing on the edge of the pavement, looking up at Nightwing Towers.

The block rose into the sky like a strange, grey watchtower. Dark birds circled above the roof. The more he stared at Nightwing Towers, the more uneasy Charlie felt about the place.

It was the last block of flats on the estate.

"I live on the second floor all alone now," said Great-aunt Sybil. "There are still a few families on the ground floor."

"Who lives on the floors above?" he asked.

"Nobody lives on the floors above," said Great-aunt Sybil. "*Nobody*."

Charlie screwed up his eyes and gazed along the top floor balcony. The flats looked empty. He thought he saw one of the birds land on the balcony edge. Then, a moment later, a figure dressed in black seemed to stand there instead. Charlie blinked, and the figure vanished. He felt the hairs on the nape of his neck bristle. As they walked towards Nightwing Towers, the girl in the baseball cap stood on the corner and watched them carefully, in silence.

# Chapter Two

Great-aunt Sybil's flat seemed very dark. She had drawn all the curtains, and continued to wear her sunglasses and scarf. She showed Charlie his room and helped him unpack. He took out his wash-bag, comb and a small mirror.

"No mirrors, please!" cried his aunt suddenly. "I don't allow them in the house!"

"Why ever not?" he began.

"Why don't you go out and play?" his aunt suggested. She threw a towel over the mirror. "I need to lie down for a bit. I'm feeling rather strange again – it's the sunshine."

Charlie followed his aunt out into the hall. She disappeared into the darkness

of her bedroom and closed the door. He scratched his head. On the wall was a photograph of Great-aunt Sybil at the seaside wearing a "Kiss-Me-Quick" hat. Sadly, he remembered how she used to be. He stared at the picture as he emptied his pockets on to the hall table. Finding the cards from the choc-ices, he slid them under the lip of the frame so that he wouldn't lose them.

Then he put
on a clean pair of jeans
and decided to get himself
a drink. As he entered the
kitchen he heard a scuffling
outside the window,
followed by footsteps.

Charlie ran out on to the balcony. The small girl he had seen in the shop shot past the door. Then, she stopped and leant over the balcony. An enormous dark bird was hovering in the air a little way off. Suddenly, it made a strange cry and soared upwards. She craned her neck to see where it had gone.

"I bet he's gone to the top floor," she said.

Charlie laughed. "It's only a bird!"

The girl turned on him sharply. "A bird? That was not a bird! Who are you anyway? I saw you earlier with Mrs Parsons!"

"I'm her nephew, Charlie. I live in the country, but I'm visiting for the week."

The girl stared at him for a moment, then seemed to relax.

"Thank goodness," she said. "I'm Freya and I live downstairs."

"What was that then, if it wasn't a bird?" asked Charlie.

"That was Mr Kube." She gave him a friendly smile. "And to think I was afraid I might have to battle against the Powers of Darkness all on my own!"

# *Chapter Three*

The late afternoon sun threw long shadows into the stairwell of Nightwing Towers. They shimmered like trembling fingers. The building felt as cool as an ancient tomb. Charlie and Freya crouched beneath the stairs on the first floor, staring down at the lift door.

Suddenly, the twang of the lift cable echoed in the shaft.

"This is it, now shush," said Freya. "The lift's coming. That will be Mr Kube. He likes to fly up to the top floor, but he sometimes uses the lift to come back down."

Charlie couldn't understand what she meant by "fly up". He held his breath as the lift door opened with a "clunk".

A man dressed in a long black cloak, wearing dark glasses very like Charlie's aunt's, peered round the door. Then he stepped out. He wore a yellow straw boater with a wide black hatband;

beneath a white collar was a smart bow-tie.

Charlie watched in wonder. The man's face was whiter than talcum powder.

Slowly, he made his way towards the entrance. Then he paused, checking that there was nobody about.

Suddenly, he stretched out his arms and flapped his cloak. A puff of smoke came from nowhere. After a few seconds, in his place was a small black animal. It squealed and stretched its wide skeletal wings. As it flew upwards Charlie realized it was a bat. In an instant it had gone.

"That was a man," gasped Charlie. "And he changed into a bat!"

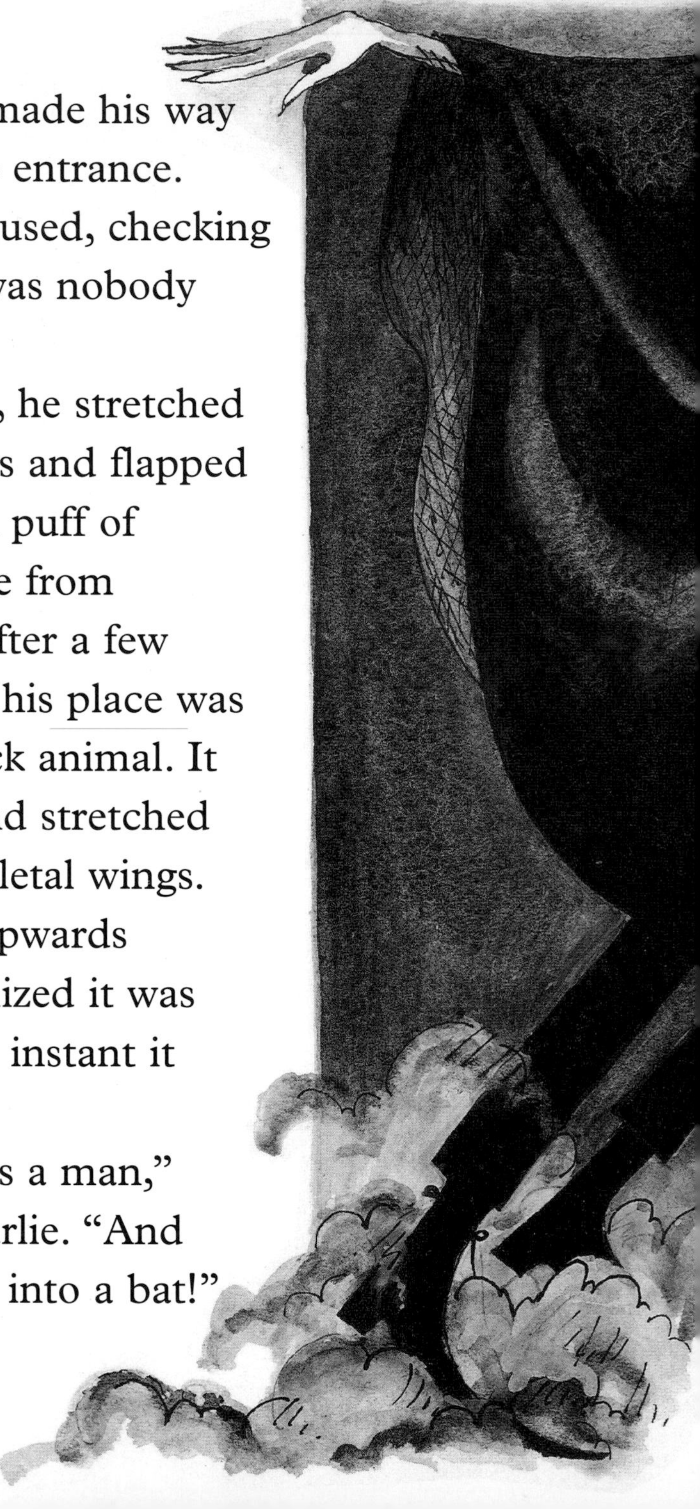

“Correction,” said Freya seriously, “that was no man, that was a Master Vampire.”

Charlie was almost speechless, but he could not deny his own eyes. Freya went on to explain that Mr Kube had only moved in a few months ago. She had watched the removals van arrive. There had been no furniture, only a collection of fine mahogany coffins.

For a moment Charlie's blood turned to iced water. He shook his head.

"No! There's no such thing as vampires!"

"OK, I'll give you further proof," she said. "But then you *must* help me. In a while Mr Kube will have returned to his flat."

# Chapter Four

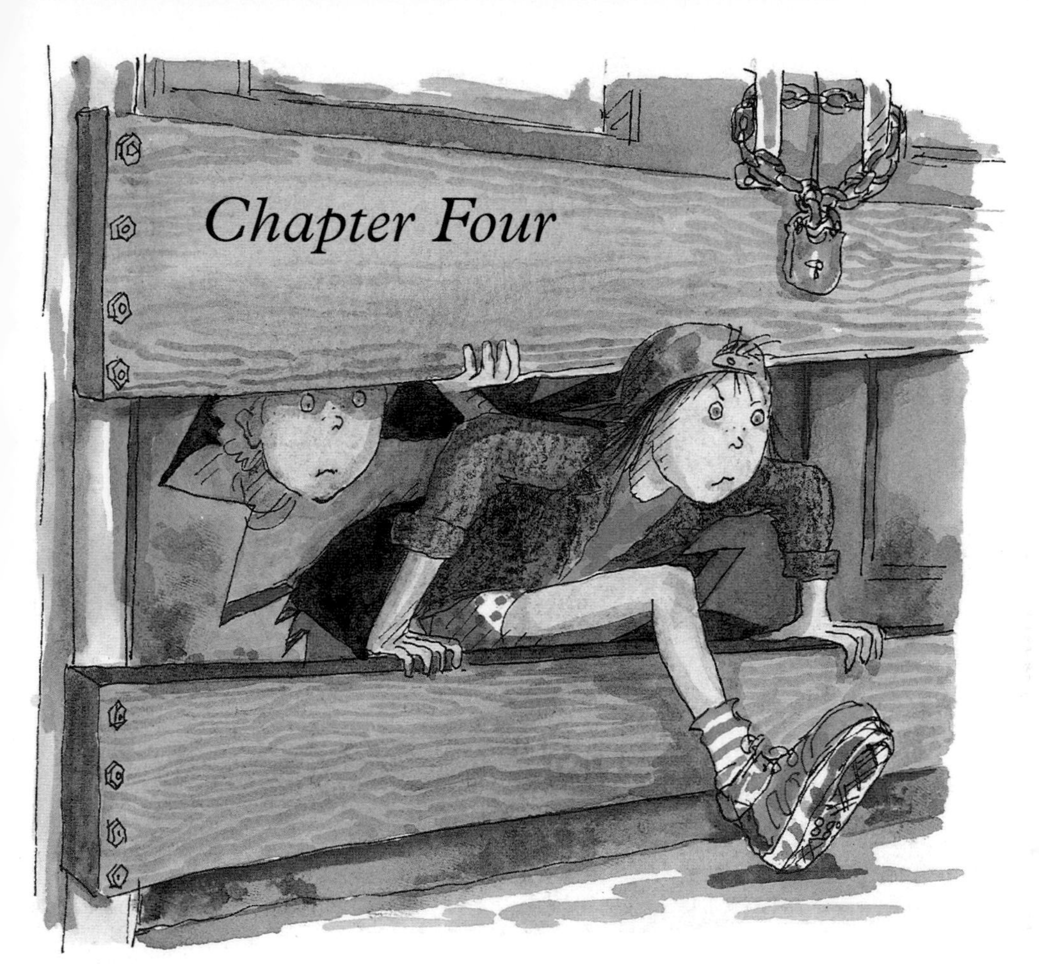

Some time later, Charlie followed Freya through the gap in the boarded-up doors which led to the third floor. Here there was another staircase. The place felt like a huge empty castle. Their footsteps rang out as they slowly climbed the stairs to the top.

"This way," said Freya when they'd reached the top floor. "Slowly and quietly." Bats hung from the ceiling like fat umbrellas. She led him out on to the balcony on tiptoe.

Most of the windows and doors were boarded, but there were two that were not.

She peered through the first window and whispered. "He's returned." She beckoned to Charlie. A grubby curtain had been drawn, but there was a gap. The room was empty, dark and silent, but in the centre was a coffin. A yellow straw hat lay on the chest of a sleeping figure, which rose and fell with each breath.

"Other single people like your aunt lived on the second floor," Freya whispered, then she moved closer to him. "Then they started to change."

Charlie's eyes widened, "*Change*?" he said.

Despite the warmth of the summer day he began to shiver.

"Mr Kube has hidden them somewhere until he is ready to command them to do his bidding. That is what Master Vampires like Dracula and Mr Kube do. The spell can only be broken by the death of the Master Vampire," said Freya. "Only then will they return to their normal state."

Suddenly, it hit Charlie.

"But, my aunt has changed, she wears dark glasses, and she's become pale and thin..."

"Exactly!" said Freya. "She is the last person living on the second floor. Why do you think I've been collecting these cards in the Dracula's Delight series? I need to find out what to do before it's too late!"

Charlie gulped and turned away. He moved along from Freya and glanced in the window of the next door flat. At first he could not believe his eyes and moved his face nearer the window.

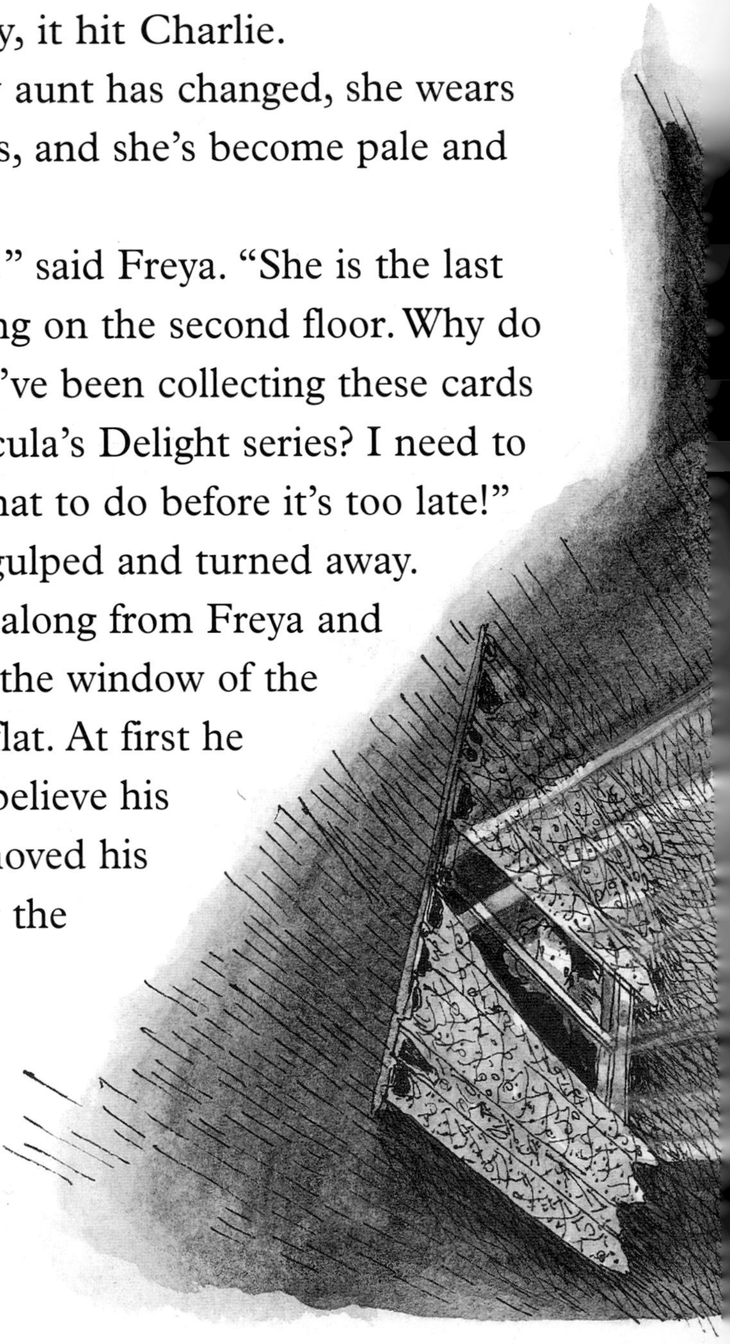

In a neat row was a line of six coffins. Five were occupied with figures in deep, deep sleep, and one, lined with purple satin, was empty.

"Look!" he said.

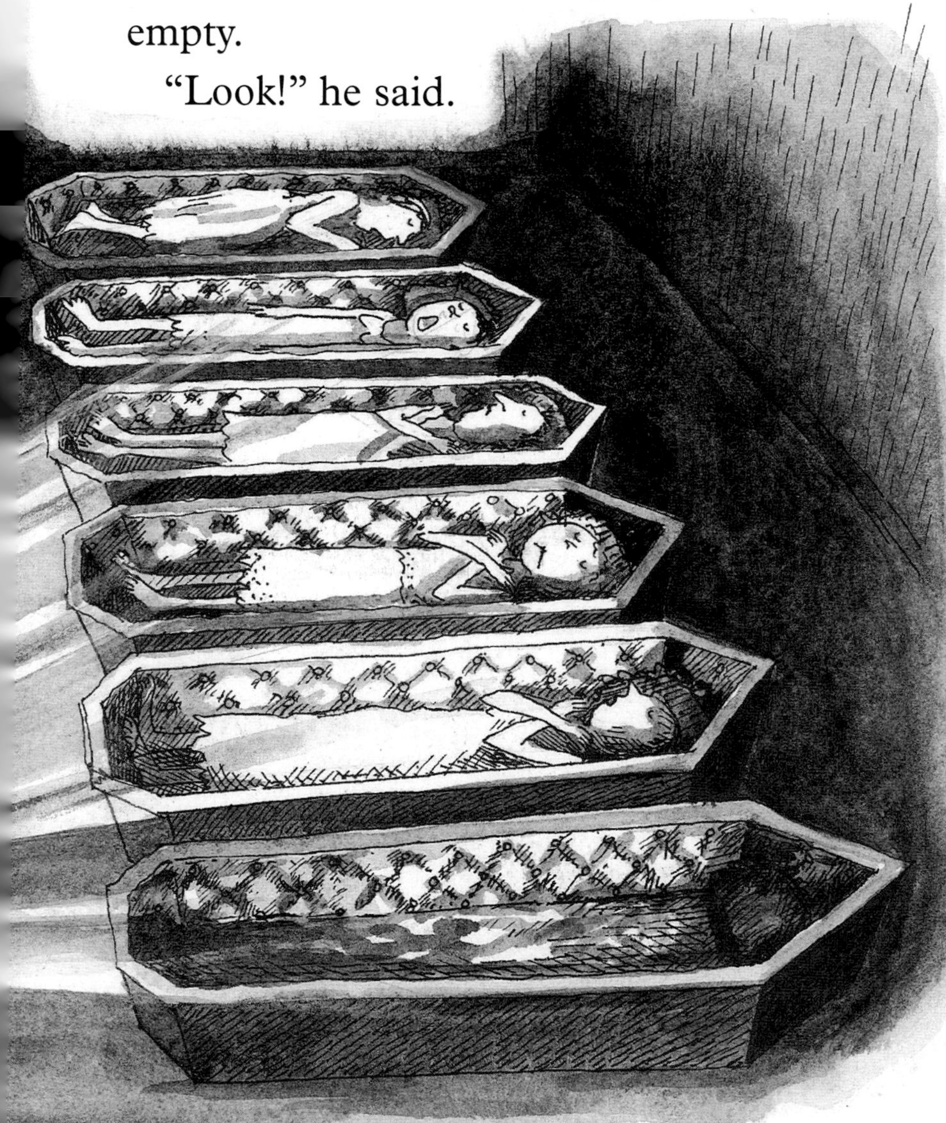

Freya rushed to his side.

"So that's where the previous tenants went! This must be where he hides his victims until he is ready. Do you see that empty coffin?" asked Freya.

Charlie nodded.

"I bet that's for your aunt," she said. "I wish I knew what to do. There's one more card in the Dracula's Delight series – that's the one that explains how to get rid of vampires."

Charlie remembered the crisp twenty-pound note his mother had given him and had an idea.

# *Chapter Five*

When he got back from the newsagent's, Great-aunt Sybil was still in her room. Freya was sitting on the balcony. Charlie gave her the big cardboard box he was carrying.

"I've bought every choc-ice in the shop," he said. "The last card must be here."

An hour later Charlie and Freya sat together at the end of the balcony surrounded by a pile of Dracula's Delight ice-cream wrappers. They had still not found the final card.

That night Charlie dreamt of old castles, set on misty mountains. Of towers with tiny windows like eyes, into which bats silently flew. In his dream he flew towards one of the windows, and as he got nearer and nearer, the castle dissolved and reappeared as Nightwing Towers. His heart beat like a hammer. Thud! Thud! Thud!

Charlie cried out with a start, and glanced at his bedside clock, it was past midnight. Someone was banging on the front door.

Charlie rushed out of his bedroom and stumbled down the passage-way. Through the frosted glass he saw Freya's outline urgently beating at the door. He opened the door wide. She stood trembling in the moonlight.

"Look behind you!" she pointed past him. "I've been keeping watch. He flew in through the window!"

Charlie turned on his heels. Great-aunt Sybil's door was ajar. From the room came the sound of horrible menacing laughter. Mr Kube pushed open the door. A long black cape billowed behind him. His face was shining milky-white in the moonlight, bigger and brighter than before. But most frightening of all, his eyes were intense and fierce.

Mr Kube's mouth yawned wide. He hissed, displaying a pair of white pointed teeth.

Freya stared desperately about her. Then her eyes fell on the old photograph of Great-aunt Sybil which hung on the wall. The two yellow choc-ice cards were still fixed in the frame.

"Charlie!" she cried. "That's the one!"

She rushed to the picture and read the back of one of the cards. For a moment she hesitated, then dived into the kitchen.

Great-aunt Sybil stood beside Mr Kube as if she were in a trance. A shaft of silver moonlight beamed through the front doorway. She no longer wore sunglasses, and her eyes were points of fire, just like his. Two puncture marks showed on her neck, the scarf had gone. She was almost transformed.

Charlie raised his hands in horror.

"She is mine!" said Mr Kube. He spat the words like snake venom. "I've come to collect."

Then suddenly, from out of the kitchen came Freya. For a moment Charlie couldn't believe his eyes. She held a toaster in her hands. With a cry of victory she ran at Mr Kube and held the toaster up to his face!

Mr Kube stared at the toaster, his jaw dropped and his eyes grew wide in disbelief.

A wail, long and dreadful, rushed around the room before disappearing into the floor below. Mr Kube crumpled like a rag, and collapsed into a heap of empty clothes.

Charlie rushed forward and kicked the cloak with his foot. There was nothing left, but a pile of grey cinders, and a twirling cloud of steam.

# *Chapter Six*

Charlie and Freya sat quietly with Great-aunt Sybil, each had an ice-cream. Several bars of semi-melted Dracula's Delight lay on the table.

"There was a whole list of ways to kill vampires: wooden stakes, cloves of garlic and so on, but I chose the first method," explained Freya.

Charlie read the card again, hardly believing that he'd had the solution to the problem all along:

*"Vampires must not see their reflection. If you hold a mirror in front of a true vampire, his own image will destroy him, turning him into dust."*

"How clever," said Great-aunt Sybil with a smile.

Freya grinned at her own reflection in the bright mirror-chrome of Great-aunt Sybil's toaster.

Meanwhile, outside in the darkness, the black shapes which had been circling the roof of Nightwing Towers flew away into the night.

# DARE TO BE SCARED!

*Are you brave enough to try more titles in the Tremors series? They're guaranteed to chill your spine…*

**Play… if you dare** by Ruth Symes
Josie can hardly believe her luck when she finds the computer game at a car boot sale. "Play… if you dare," the game challenges. So she does. Further and further she plays, each level of the game scarier than the last. Then she reaches the last level. "Play… if you dare," repeats the game. But if she does, she could be trapped for ever…

**The Claygate Hound** by Jan Dean
On the school camp to Claygate, Billy is determined to scare everyone with his terrifying stories of the Claygate Hound, a vicious ghost dog said to lurk nearby. Ryan and Zeb ignore his warnings and explore the woods. They hear a ghostly howl – and run. Has Billy been speaking the truth, or is there a more terrifying reason for what they have heard?

**The Curse of the Frozen Loch** by Anthony Masters
Why does the ghostly figure skate the loch in the dead of night? And what is wrong with Great-Aunt Fiona? Will and Sarah are determined to solve the mystery and save Fiona. But will they be the next victims of the curse of the frozen loch?

**The Ghost of Golfhawk School** by Tessa Potter
Martin and Dan love frightening the younger children at school with scary ghost stories. But then Kirsty arrives. Kirsty claims that she can actually see ghosts. Then a mysterious virus sweeps through the school. Martin is still sure she is lying. After all – ghosts don't exist, do they?